To renew or order li⊦
www.lincolnsⱡ
You will require a Personal
Ask any member o

D1512821

L5/9

JN 04188504

Lost!

Helen Orme

Ransom

Lost!

by Helen Orme
Illustrated by Cathy Brett
Cover by Anna Torborg

Published by Ransom Publishing Ltd.
Rose Cottage, Howe Hill, Watlington, Oxon. OX49 5HB
www.ransom.co.uk

ISBN   978 184167 598 5

First published in 2007

Meet the Sisters ...

Siti and her friends are really close. So close she calls them her Sisters. They've been mates for ever, and most of the time they are closer than her real family.

Siti is the leader – the one who always knows what to do – but Kelly, Lu, Donna and Rachel have their own lives to lead as well.

Still, there's no one you can talk to, no one you can rely on, like your best mates. Right?

1

Looking after the little ones

"Siti!"

Siti looked at her mum.

"You'll have to look after the others today. I've got meetings all day."

Siti pulled a face. She hated having to look after the three younger ones.

"Why can't dad look after them? It's half term."

"Dad's got to go into school today."

"But I'm going shopping with the Sisters."

The Sisters were Siti's friends. They did everything together.

"Take them with you."

Siti gave in. Mum wouldn't change her mind.

She texted the Sisters.

"Got to bring little ones! C U later."

She hoped they wouldn't mind. She was the only one with three younger ones in the family. Her mum and dad were busy people and she often had to look after Daudi, Hanif and Afia.

Afia was O.K. She was only four and did what she was told. Hanif was nine and he was O.K. most of the time. But Daudi was twelve and thought he was really grown up. He was a pain. And he hated being one of the 'little ones'. Siti often called him that just to annoy him!

Her mobile beeped. It was Donna.

"No probs – we'll all help."

Donna had a younger brother. She understood.

Daudi moaned, of course.

"Why do I have to go out with her friends? Why can't I go to Jason's?"

"Because I don't trust you at Jason's," said mum. "Go with Siti and be good!"

2

Just you wait!

Daudi moaned all the way to the shopping centre. He wouldn't sit with Siti on the bus.

"Why won't mum let me go to Jason's?"

He went on and on.

"I don't like girls, I don't like your friends. They're all stupid."

"Shut up, Daudi. I don't want you with me either."

By the time they got to the shopping centre Siti was really cross with Daudi. Hanif had started moaning too.

"I want to go to the library. You lot will make me go round the shops. It's boring."

At least Afia was being good. She liked bus rides.

Siti was glad when she saw Kelly and Lu. At last, someone sensible to talk to!

"Where are the others?"

"In the shoe shop, that one over by the ice cream stall," said Kelly.

"Come on, we'll go and find them."

Hanif and Daudi looked at each other.

"Shoes!"

"Boring!" they said together.

Siti had had enough. "Oh, go to the library," she said crossly. "You can go on the Internet or something."

The boys grinned.

"I'm coming to check on you in half an hour. You'd better be there."

"Girls!" said Daudi in disgust.

"Just you wait," he said, but Siti was gone. "I'll get my own back on you."

3

Afia wants an ice cream

"Come on," said Lu. "Let's find Donna and Rachel."

Kelly held out her hand to Afia.

"Do you want to come and look at the pretty shoes?"

"I want an ice cream," said Afia, as they walked past the stall.

"Later," said Siti.

"Now!"

Afia let go of Kelly and sat down on the floor.

"Want ice cream," she said loudly.

Siti pulled her arm and tried to make her stand up.

Afia shouted even louder.

"Ice cream!"

"I'll get her one," said Kelly.

"No way," said Siti. "Not when she's screaming like this. Come on, leave her here – she'll follow us in a minute."

Siti headed into the shoe shop. Kelly and Lu followed her.

"Will she be all right?" asked Kelly.

"Yeah, she does this all the time. If she doesn't come in a minute, I'll go out again."

Just then, Rachel saw them and rushed over to show off her new shoes.

"Where next?" asked Donna.

"I want a skirt and top," said Lu. "Let's go to that new shop. They've got some really good stuff."

"No, let's go to the food hall," said Kelly.

"What do you want to go there for?" asked Siti. "It's too early to eat."

Donna laughed. "I know – I saw Simon and Gary down there!"

Siti laughed. She knew that once Kelly

had seen Gary she would want to go and hang out where he would see her.

Then she looked round. There was no sign of Afia. She ran outside, expecting to see Afia still sitting on the floor.

She got outside and stopped. Afia was gone!

4

'She can't have gone far'

Siti called her name and the others ran out.

"Don't worry, she can't have gone far," said Donna.

"Let's split up and search," said Siti. "I'll look round here. Donna, can you and Lu go downstairs please."

"We'll do the top floor," said Rachel. "What sort of shops does she like?"

"Meet back here in ten minutes," said Siti.

Siti went to talk to the girl on the ice cream stand. She'd noticed Afia at first – it would have been hard not to see the small, loud child shouting for ice cream, but then she'd got busy and hadn't seen her again.

Siti was beginning to get really scared by the time she met up with the others.

"We're going to have to tell someone," she said. "Where do you report lost children?"

"Security guards," said Kelly. "They might have something on CCTV."

They rushed off to look for a security guard. Siti began to explain what had happened. The guard listened carefully.

"Don't worry," he said kindly. "Kids that age are always getting lost here. I'll take you to the office. You never know, they might already have her there."

For a few minutes Siti cheered up, but there were no lost children in the office.

She suddenly felt really sick.

The guard explained to the man in the office. "We'll put out a lost child call," he said.

"What's that?" asked Siti.

"A message to all the floors," he said. "What does your sister look like and what's she wearing?"

Siti told him and soon they heard the message asking anyone who had seen Afia to come to the office.

A couple of women arrived. "We've seen a girl like that," they said. "It was by the ice cream stall. She was crying. She was being dragged off by a couple of boys."

5

'What am I going to tell mum?'

Siti felt even sicker. She looked at the faces of the people around. They looked worried too.

"Have you got the CCTV tapes, Harry?" asked the guard.

"I'll get them now." He went off.

The girls looked at each other. Siti was nearly crying. "What am I going to tell mum?"

Soon Harry was back with a video tape. He put it in the machine.

"This is from the nearest camera."

He went through the tape at high speed. Then something showed up on the screen.

It was a little girl sitting on the floor. Siti, Kelly and Lu were there.

"That's us," said Kelly.

They saw themselves go off and leave Afia. The guard looked at them hard.

"Why did you leave her? That was a stupid thing to do."

Siti started to explain, but stopped when Harry said "Look!"

On screen Afia was standing up. A boy
was pulling on her arm and she was trying
to push him away.

Another, smaller, boy appeared and started
to drag her other arm.

The smaller boy turned towards the camera.

"Hanif!" gasped Siti.

6

No answer

"Do you know those lads?"

"They're my brothers."

"Why didn't they come when we asked people to contact us?"

Siti shrugged. "Dunno."

She got out her mobile and rang Daudi. There was no answer.

"Maybe something's happened to them too," she said.

"I think we need to get your parents," said Harry.

Siti gave him the school phone number. It wasn't long before her dad arrived.

Siti was so glad to see him that she really did burst into tears.

"I don't know where they are. I'm so sorry. I didn't leave her for long and I thought the boys were safe."

"Have you tried to ring Daudi?" said her dad.

"Yes but his mobile's off."

"Have you tried home?"

Siti shook her head.

Dad got out his mobile and rang.

Siti watched her dad's face. There was no answer.

7

Police, quickly!

Dad looked grim. He turned to Harry.

"What do we do now?"

"Police," said Harry. "Quickly."

Harry moved towards the phone. As he put out his hand it rang.

He picked it up and listened. "Bring them up," he said.

"I think we've found them. They were coming in through the main entrance."

They didn't have to wait long, but it seemed like forever to Siti.

Dad looked sternly at Daudi and Hanif.

"What do you two think you're playing at?" he asked. "Why didn't you come to the office before? Where have you been?"

Daudi grinned.

"We came and got Afia. She was crying so we took her to the park."

He turned to Siti. "You didn't look after her, so we did. She had a great time with us."

Dad looked from Daudi to Siti.

"Home." he said. "I think you've both got some explaining to do – don't you?"